THIS WALKER BOOK BELONGS TO:

_____

_____

_____

For Josie and Oliver

First published 1995 by Walker Books Ltd
87 Vauxhall Walk, London SE11 5HJ

This edition including DVD published 2008

2 4 6 8 10 9 7 5 3 1

© 1995 Lucy Cousins

The right of Lucy Cousins to be identified as author/illustrator of this work has been
asserted by her in accordance with the Copyright, Designs and Patents Act 1988

Lucy Cousins font © 1995 Lucy Cousins

Printed in China

British Library Cataloguing in Publication Data:
a catalogue record for this book is available from the British Library

ISBN 978-1-4063-1543-1

Za-Za's
Baby Brother

Lucy Cousins

WALKER BOOKS

AND SUBSIDIARIES

LONDON · BOSTON · SYDNEY · AUCKLAND

My mum is going to have a baby.

She has a big fat tummy. There's not much room for a cuddle.

Granny came to look after me.

Dad took mum to
the hospital.

When the baby was born we went to see Mum.

When Mum came home she was very tired. I had to be very quiet and help Dad look after her.

All my uncles and aunts came to see the baby.

I played on my own.

Dad was always busy.

Mum was always busy.

"Dad, Will you read me a story?"
"Not now, Za-za. We're going shopping soon."

"Mum, can we go to the toyshop?"

"Sorry, Za-za, baby's hungry and we have to go home."

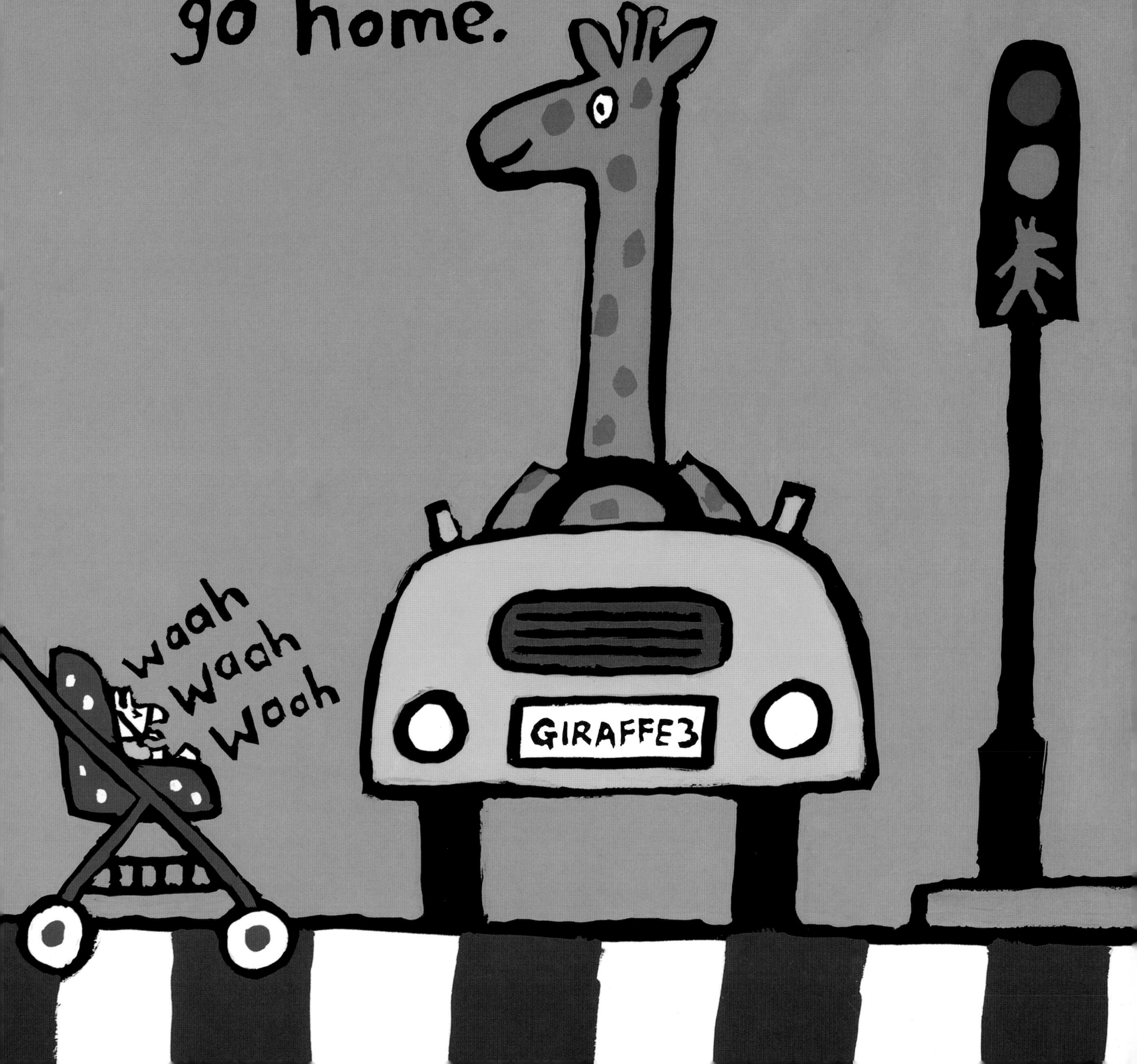

"Can I have my tea soon?"

"Yes, Za-za."

"Mum! I want a cuddle **NOW!**"

"Why don't you cuddle the baby?"

So I cuddled the baby...

and I pushed him...

and I built him a tower.

He was nice. It was fun.

When the baby got tired Mum put him to bed.

Then I got my
cuddle...

and a bedtime story.